THE BACKPACKS WITH FEET

CHARLOTTE DUNCAN-WAGNER

DEDICATION

I dedicate my book to my parents. They gave me the love of books and listened to me read aloud from the "See Johnny Run" book series. My father challenged me to write my own books in 2001. Thank you Daddy for reminding me that I have stories to tell. I am a writer. My parents' love encourages me still.

Calvin George Duncan 1921-2005, Dottie B. Duncan 1918 -1991

ACKNOWLEDGEMENT

Thank you to all: Pete Ferguson, Thomas Christie, Elliott Elementary, and Lincoln Public Schools for the opportunity to serve as a Community Greeter. My life was enriched by the many languages spoken by the students. Sylvia Franklin for the initial feedback needed to germinate project. Charlene Maxey-Harris and your band of librarians whose critique allowed me to fine-tune and focus the dialogue. Carrie and Willie Banks, your priceless classroom and reading curriculum expertise has validated this book as a source to encourage listening to construct meaning and connect ideas. Moses T. Alexander Greene my writing teach, mentor, proofreader, and friend. There are many people who listened to the story and served as focus groups across the country to give me feedback and fill out my survey. Aletta McClendon and April Stone who asked how the book was coming along so their children can read it. Special appreciation to the illustrator Jerry L. Washington Jr. Your drawings and my words will live forever. Bless you my friend. To my creative family: Annie Bloomfield, Otto Green Jr., Bobbye Jean Wagner, Minister Jason Wagner II, Dr. Aundria Green, my husband Jason Wagner Sr. you inspire me with your talents, you encourage me, you cheer for me, and you affirm me. I love you. Thank you God for answered prayer, publishing my first book.

Reader's Notes: The Backpacks with Feet is a read aloud book. The book can be personalized by inserting the name of the school and street as a replacement for "at **your school on that street**".

Example: at Elliott School on 25th St.

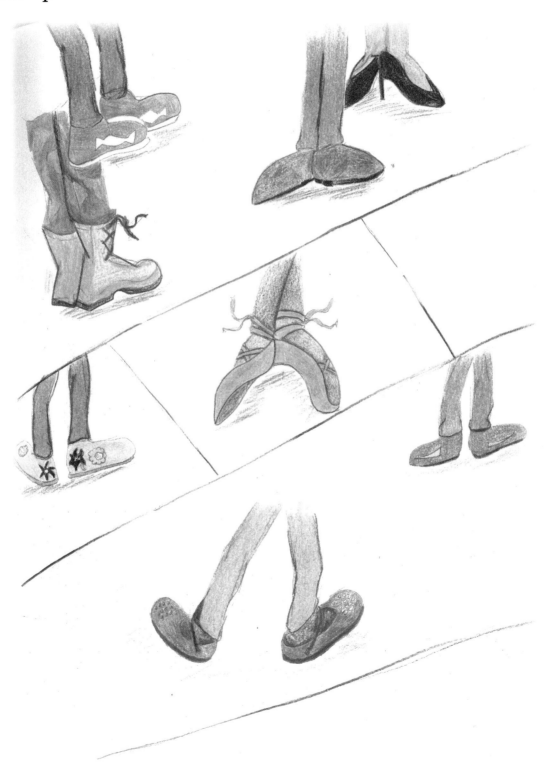

Alex Brown lived across the street *from your school on that street*. Each Friday he waved to everyone that walked past the big front room window of his family's house.

"Good morning teachers. Good morning parents. Good morning Backpacks with Feet," Alex said.

"Hello." "Good morning." "Hi." Someone would say in response.

"Was that you walking?"

Each Friday Alex's Mama would set an extra plate at the dining table.

Alex's Grandpa J. came for breakfast one day a week before he went to volunteer ***at your school on that street.***

Grandpa J. laughed and chewed food with his mouth open on Fridays. He did not walk slowly on Fridays. Grandpa J. ate fast on Fridays.

Grandpa J. said a quick thank you to Alex's Mama and hurried outside to wait. Grandpa J. and the other greeters were weekly volunteers for the school's Weekend Backpack Program. They sorted groceries and stuffed bags of fresh fruit and boxed food to hand out to students *at your school on that street*.

Mama waved as Grandpa J., leaning on his cane, called from the edge of the sidewalk to Alex. Alex ran down the steps trying to reach the cross walk with the Backpacks with Feet.

"Alex, please don't talk to strangers," his Mama said every week.

"They will not be strangers anymore," Alex said. "I am the star greeter with Grandpa J."

Alex was too late to join the sidewalk parade with the teachers, parents, and Backpacks with Feet. He obeyed the crossing guard and crossed safely, ***to your school on that street.*** The sidewalk parade made a tour around the school yard just as Alex met up with Grandpa J. and the other volunteer greeters for door A, B, and C.

As Alex neared the school house steps, he could hear many voices laughing, talking, and whispering in many languages. Was that you talking?

"Good morning," Alex said as he stepped aside to usher Group 1 into the door for the morning assembly.

"Buenos Dias," Alex said as he stepped aside for Group 2; the Backpacks with Feet stepped on by. Not a single Backpack with Feet gave a reply.

There were more Backpacks with Feet bumping in and out of the ziggy zaggy lines waiting to enter Door A, B, and C.

"Good morning to me, and you," Alex said to them.

Not one Backpack with Feet replied as they sidestepped on by.

The Backpacks with Feet wear many shoes. Purple basketball shoes with red lights, combat boots, and sandals too.

Those Backpacks with Feet wore sneakers with orange flowers, green buttons, blue shoes with lightning stripes. Some Backpacks with Feet wore sparkling ballet flats and jeweled moccasins. Are those your shoes?

Alex tried, "Xin Chao", to the Backpacks with Feet who marched in with their heads to one side. Not seeing their face, sparkling eyes or even a smile.

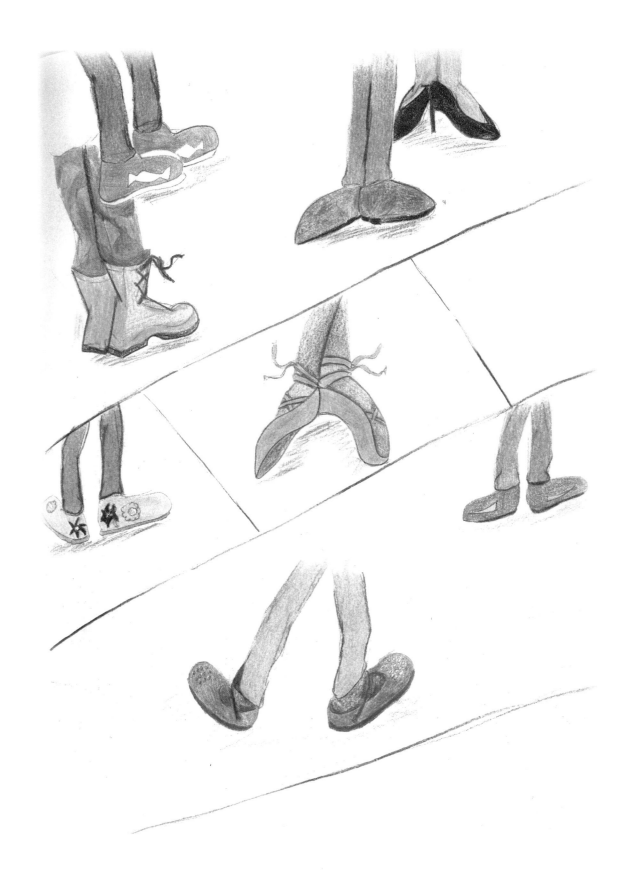

The Backpacks with Feet were silent and strong as they carried Dancing Diana, G.I. John, Weber Will, and Hillary Hilltop along.

G.I. JOHN

G.I.
JOHN

Dancing Diana

'Dancing
Diana'

Weber Will

HILLARY HILLTOP

'HILLARY HILLTOP'

Those Backpacks with Feet had curly and straight hair, beads and braids, buzz cuts and fades, and scarves and hijabs on their heads.

"Assalamu alaikum," Alex said to other Backpacks with Feet who stepped on by. If some Backpacks with Feet will not speak, give it another try.

In a clear loud voice, "Wa alaikum assalaam," one Backpack with Feet replied. Then, two, three, and four, Backpacks with Feet made the choice to look up at Alex and kindly say, "Hi." "Bon jour." "Ni-Hao."

"Hola," another Backpack with Feet said to Alex with a smile.

Alex and Grandpa J. quietly closed Door A, as did each volunteer at Door B and Door C. Alex listened to the Principal give the morning announcements and heard these words; "And now welcome to the stage, our Star Greeter, 2nd grader Alex Brown, who will give us directions about the Weekend Backpack Program, and lead us in greetings and affirmations."

The gym exploded with thunderous applause as he stood in front of teachers, Grandpa J., volunteers and all of the Backpacks with Feet.

"Good morning, I am Alex Ivory Brown", he said to the smiling faces of the boys and girls **at your school on that street.**

"Good Morning, Alex" the boys and girls said in their big loud voices.

"We are told not to talk to strangers, right?" Alex asked the students.

"Well, I want to introduce my Grandpa J. who is a community volunteer with the Weekend Backpack Program. He is not a stranger." Alex said, "Always practice good manners at home and at school, like hello and thank you."

"If you see Grandpa J. around the school he may say hi, try to smile and say hi back." Alex said to the assembly **at your school on that street.**

The Backpacks with Feet kept all eyes on Alex. "Now I will lead you in the morning greetings and affirmations. After your greeting, tell everyone why you are special."

"Good morning," Alex said in his loud voice as he stood in front of the teachers, students, and volunteers **at your school on that street**. The Backpacks with Feet had many replies.

"Hola, I am somebody special because I am me," Dancing Diana said.

"Bon jour. I am somebody special because I can read", Weber Will said.

Hillary Hilltop rose from sitting to standing to proudly say,

"Good morning!!" I am somebody special because I respect myself and others."

Was that you?

'HILLARY HILLTOP'

"Gracias a todas." "Thank you everyone." Alex said.

The bell rang. The Backpacks with Feet stood in that ziggy zaggy line, ready to go to their own classrooms **at your school on that street.**

GLOSSARY

Assalamu alaikum - pronounced assa-la-mu-a-lay-koom, traditional Arabic greeting used by Muslims around the world, means peace be unto to you

Wa alaikum assalaam: pronounced wa- alaykum al--sa-lom, response to greeting means, and upon you be peace

Bonjour: pronounced bon-sure, hello in French

Buenos Dias: good day in Spanish

Greeter: someone who welcomes others upon their arrival

Hijabs: a head covering worn by some Muslim women to cover their hair and neck

Hillary Hilltop: Barbara Hillary 1931- First Female African American to reach the North Pole

Hola: pronounced Oh lah, hello in Spanish

Ni-hao: pronounced nee-how, hello in Mandarin Chinese

Positive: focusing on good things rather than bad

Special: unique to a specific person or thing

Volunteer: someone who helps because it makes them happy

Xin-chao: pronounced seen chow, hello everyone in Vietnamese